Ankle Soup

Written by Maureen Sullivan   Illustrated by Alison Josephs

xo Alison

MoJo InkWorks™

MoJo InkWorks™

MoJo InkWorks is a children's press.

Text copyright © 2008 by Maureen Sullivan

Illustrations copyright © 2008 by Alison Josephs

Printed in the U.S.A.

Carlos the Dog™ and Carlos the French Bulldog™ are trademarks of MoJo InkWorks.

Macy's Thanksgiving Day Parade images courtesy of Macy's.

For information contact
Maureen Sullivan, MoJo InkWorks,
16 Foxglove Row, Riverhead, NY 11901-1216
Phone: 212-243-0732
www.anklesoup.com www.mojoinkworks.com

Library of Congress Control Number: 2008907382
Sullivan, Maureen. ISBN 978-0-9820381-0-9. First Edition.

For Tara, my first, and Carlos, hers.
Great ankles.

MNS

For Leah and Barry who taught me to reach for the stars,
and to Ruby for keeping me grounded.

AJ

I never know
what my mistress is doing.
She has a routine
that she's always pooh-poohing.
The way that things change
make me jumpy and nervous.
Could it be she's an agent?
F.B.I.?
Secret Service?

So let me describe
what happened one day.
It was fall in New York,
the parade underway.
My mistress and I
rushed out of the door,
and jumped in a cab
fearing soon it might pour.

We stopped at a building
with a fancy-pants portal
and a winged-superhero,
Mercury the Immortal!
It was Grand Central Station
on Thanksgiving Day.
Would you check out this crowd?
Ay Caramba!
Oy Vey!

The whiffs that I sniffed
at the Grand Central shops,
were driving me crazy,
had me licking my chops.
Chopped liver and garlic,
sharp cheeses and curry,
careened then combined
in a torturous flurry.

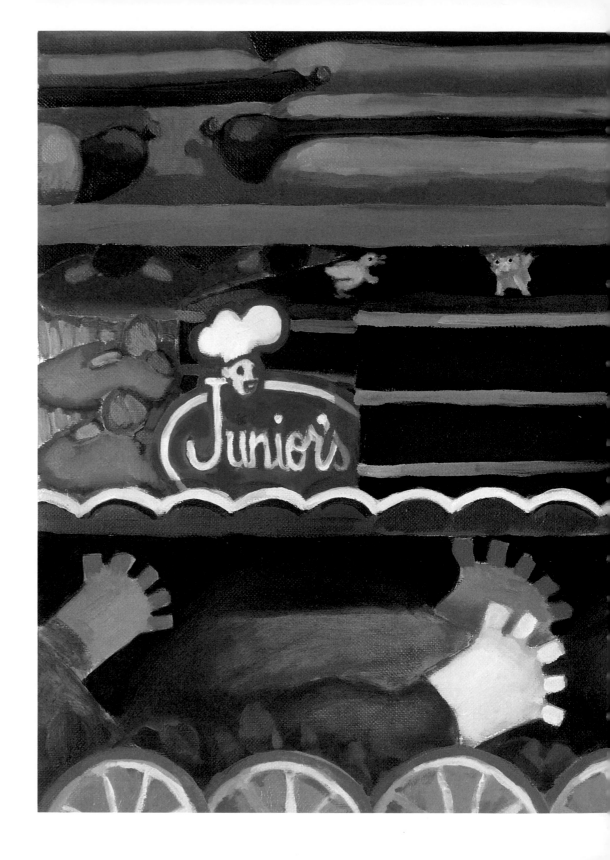

My mistress was meeting
her sister and brother,
her sister's beau, Scott,
and her Long Island mother.
To head off with me
on the Metro North train,
for turkey with friends
and to drink their champagne.

The ceiling above
was a heavenly stew
of planets and galaxies
awash in green-blue.
Beneath a young woman,
running fast to her gate,
fell into the arms
of her tall, handsome mate.

I spied a Great Dane
with paws big as pies,
his mouth five feet wide
and gi-normous eyes.
Dropping more than a globule
of slithery drool,
it crashed like Niagara
and left quite a pool.

I smelled that great smell
of shoes that were old,
worn by a man
who looked hungry
and cold.
A kindly gent bent
as he peeled from a wad,
a spanking new twenty
with a smile and a nod.

Making their way
through the zig-zagging crowd,
was a lady and guide dog,
of whom she seemed proud…
dodging the throng
of people and things,
unfazed by distractions
the holiday brings.

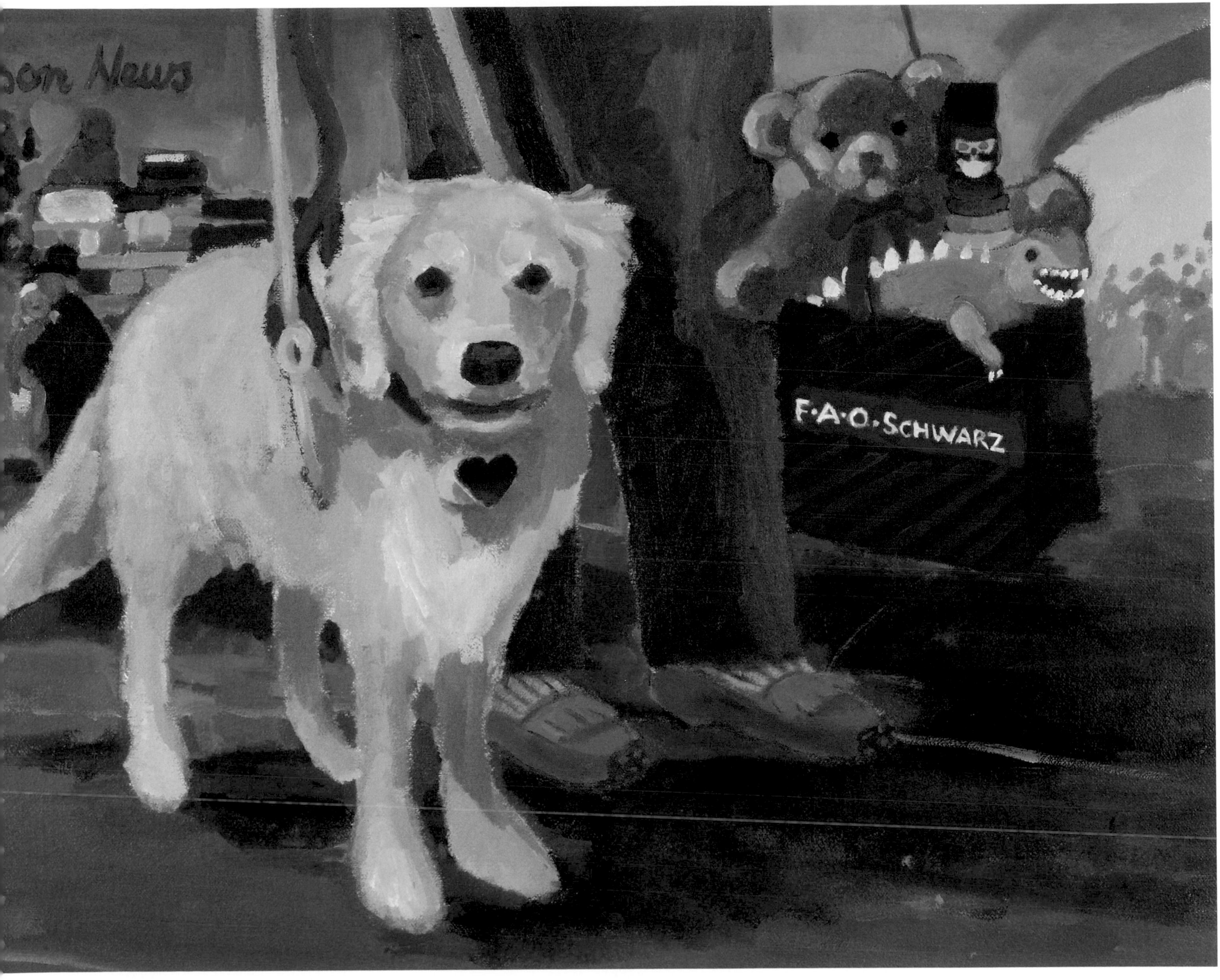

son News
F·A·O·SCHWARZ

Toting bags full of treats
were four ladies from China.
In soft silken slippers
they couldn't look finer.
I hoped that their dinner
would bring them good luck.
Can you Peking a turkey,
or only a duck?

Next came six feet
that were little and sweet.
A bandy-legged insect?
No,
triplets who greet
their grandmother waiting,
who smiles when she sees,
this threesome of ladies
as tall as her knees.

To grandma they're little,
to me they are big.
A French Bulldog named Carlos,
I look like a pig.
I feel like an ant
in a giraffe-ic group,
when I look straight ahead,
it's **all** ankle soup.

So smile when you see me
way down in the crowd.
And bend to my level
for crying out loud!
Please try to see things
from my point of view.
Your ankles are nice but…
you're *more* than a shoe.

Rich and poor, short and tall

We're in it together on this great big ball

Let's all be grateful on this Thanksgiving Day

For the soup we're all in and life's buffet

The End

Special thanks to:

Educational specialists Ann Donohue, Jean McPadden and Katie Mullaney
for their scholarly advice, encouragement and friendship.

David Josephs and Alan Ginsberg for their wise counsel.